WIMEE'S WORDS

WIMEE LEARNS
ABOUT MONEY

FRESHLY
50¢ SQUEEZED 50¢
LEMONADE!

Bike
TODAY $1.00

WRITTEN BY
STEPHANIE KAMMERAAD
CREATED BY
MICHAEL HYACINTHE
KEVIN KAMMERAAD

ZONDERkidz

For the Dague family—your two cents are always priceless!

—SK and KK

To Nia, Mya, Lucas, and Blake—love, earn, give.

—MH

To my beloved Delia and Vittoria, may your
future be as bright as your smile.

—MC

ZONDERKIDZ

Wimee Learns About Money
Copyright © 2024 by Wimage, LLC
Illustrations © 2024 by Wimage, LLC

Requests for information should be addressed to:

Zonderkidz, 3900 *Sparks Drive, Grand Rapids, Michigan* 49546

Hardcover ISBN 978-0-310-15361-0
Ebook ISBN 978-0-310-15362-7

Library of Congress Cataloging-in-Publication Data

Names: Kammeraad, Stephanie, author. | Cerato, Mattia, illustrator.
Title: Wimee learns about money / by Stephanie Kammeraad ; interior
   illustration, Mattia Cerato.
Description: Grand Rapids, Michigan : Zonderkidz, [2024] | Series: A
   Wimee's Words book | "Created by Kevin Kammeraad and Michael Hyacinthe"
   | Audience: Ages 4-8. | Summary: When Wimee the robot receives some
   coins from his grandmother and learns what money is--and all about
   earning, spending, and saving it--the information comes in handy when he
   is invited to a beach party.
Identifiers: LCCN 2022056886 (print) | LCCN 2022056887 (ebook) | ISBN
   9780310153610 (hardcover) | ISBN 9780310153627 (ebook)
Subjects: LCSH: Readers (Primary) | LCGFT: Readers (Publications)
Classification: LCC PE1119.2 .K365 2024 (print) | LCC PE1119.2 (ebook) |
   DDC 428.6/2--dc23/eng/20230403
LC record available at https://lccn.loc.gov/2022056886
LC ebook record available at https://lccn.loc.gov/2022056887

Illustrations: Mattia Cerato
Editor: Katherine Jacobs
Design and art direction: Cindy Davis

Printed in India

24 25 26 27 28 /REP/ 14 13 12 11 10 9 8 7 6 5 4 3 2 1

Wimee was excited. He had just received a card in the mail from his grandmother.

Wimee, congratulations on your first gear upgrade!

Your future is looking bright!

Love, Grandma

Inside were pieces of green paper with numbers and faces on them. He wondered what they were.

Maybe my friends will know what these are, Wimee thought.
He headed outside to find Moby and Siblee.

Moby and Siblee were at the park. "Hi, Wimee!" they called. They were with their new friend, Sylvia, showing her the fountain. Wimee hurried over.

They all loved seeing the water splash and spray up and down. There were small glistening circles under the water.

"What are those?" Sylvia wondered aloud.

Their neighbor, Mr. Bill, was standing nearby. "Those are coins, a kind of money. There are different types of coins and each one has a different value," explained Mr. Bill.

"I like how shiny they are," Moby said.

"They're shiny because they are made of metal. Money comes in the form of paper too, but that wouldn't work to throw into a fountain!" Mr. Bill laughed.

"Oh, is that what these pieces of paper are?" Wimee asked, showing Mr. Bill the card from his grandma.

Wimee's friends leaned in to see. Mr. Bill nodded. "Those are called bills," he said.

"What do I do with them?" Wimee asked.

"Great question!" said Mr. Bill. "Money is used to buy things you need, such as groceries, or things you want, like a kite.

When you get money, you can spend it to buy things right away,

save it in order to buy things later,

or you can give it to others so that they can buy things they need or want."

"Then why do people throw the coin money into the water?" asked Wimee.

"Wishes," said Mr. Bill. "Some people believe that if you throw a coin into a fountain and make a wish, the wish will come true."

"Oh! I want some blueberry-popcorn-flavored ice cream!" announced Siblee. "Can I wish for money to buy some?"

"Yes, you can," said Mr. Bill, "but that doesn't mean the wish will come true. You usually get money by earning it, investing it, or receiving it as a gift."

"Like in this card I got from my grandmother!" Wimee said excitedly, holding out the bills.

"How can Siblee, Sylvia, and I get some money, Mr. Bill?"
Moby asked.

"Well," said Mr. Bill, "one way to earn money is to sell things you make or own. Another way is to charge money for doing something for someone, like washing their bike."

Bike Wash
TODAY $1.00

"Great! Thanks, Mr. Bill!" Moby said.

On their way back home, Wimee and his friends talked about how they could earn money. "Maybe we could make lemonade and sell it," suggested Sylvia.

"Good idea!" Wimee said. "But I don't have any lemons. Do you?"

"No," each friend replied.

"Maybe we could build rhinoceros puppets and sell them at the makers' market!" exclaimed Siblee.

"That would be fun!" said Wimee. Then he remembered the next market day was a few weeks away.

"I know!" Wimee said. "Let's start a dog-walking service!" Wimee and his friends loved dogs and their neighbors had lots of them!

They got started right away.

By the end of the week, their neighbors were pleased, the dogs were tired, and the friends were delighted. They had earned a lot of money!

Wimee, Moby, Siblee, and Sylvia set off to the store together. Wimee looked up and down every aisle. Finally, he saw exactly what he wanted.

He took it to the register and used his money to buy it. To his surprise, he still had money left over!

When he got home, Wimee put his leftover money into two jars. Remembering what Mr. Bill had said, Wimee decided to save some for the next time he needed or wanted something.

He also wanted to use some money to help others.

The next morning, Wimee met Moby, Siblee, and Sylvia at the park.

"We learned so much about money this week," said Wimee.
"I wonder what we'll learn about next!"

Wimee and his friends learned a lot about money.
You can learn about it too!

What is money?

Money is what people exchange for goods and services. That means that you can trade money for things such as ice cream, like Siblee wanted in the story, or groceries, like Mr. Bill needed. You can also trade money for doing work such as walking dogs, like Wimee and his friends did.

Money comes in the form of coins and bills. Coins are circular and made of metal. Bills are rectangular and are made of special paper.

Different countries have different kinds of money, or currencies. The currency in the United States is the US Dollar. Money has a set value everyone accepts. For example, one dollar has a value of 100 cents. Look at the charts below—they show the values of money in the United States.

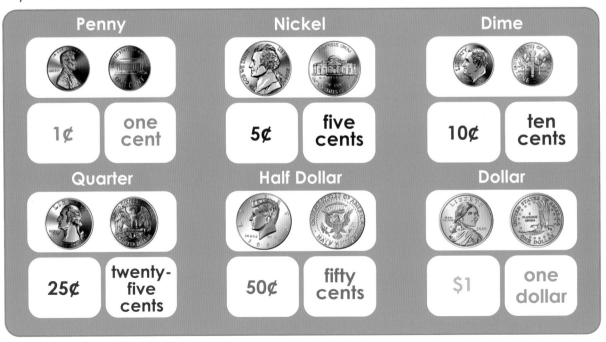

One Dollar $1

Five Dollars $5

Ten Dollars $10

Twenty Dollars $20

Fifty Dollars $50

One Hundred Dollars $100

How do you get money?

There are several ways to get money. Wimee and his friends learned about this from Mr. Bill.

One way to get money is as a gift, like when Wimee received money from his grandma.

Another way to get money is to earn it. Earn means to get paid for doing some type of work. Wimee and his friends earned money walking dogs for their neighbors. Other jobs kids might do are raking their neighbors' leaves, babysitting, or doing chores at home. Adults earn money by working at their jobs.

Kids and adults can get money by selling things they make or own—like when Wimee and his friends talked about a lemonade stand.

You can also get money by investing. Investing means you put money where it can grow or make more. One common way to invest is by buying part of a business. This is called a share. When the business does well, it makes more money. That means whoever owns a share of the business has their money grow too! Companies then give money back to the people who own shares in the company throughout the year.

What can you do with money?

Wimee and his friends learned that when you get money, you can spend it by buying things right away, save it in order to buy things later, or you can give it to others so they can buy things they need or want.

Where do you store money?

When Wimee had money he wanted to save, he put it in jars at home. This is a great place to put your money when you start saving it, and you can use any empty container you have. Some kids even have piggy banks!

Another place you can keep your money is at a financial institution like a bank or a credit union. You protect your money and help it grow by opening up a checking or savings account. By depositing your money into an account, the financial institution holds it for you until you need it.

If you open a checking account, you don't need to carry coins or dollar bills in order to spend money. You can spend the money you have by using a debit card. The card is made out of plastic. It has all of the information that computers need to know, including how much money is in your account. Some people who have checking accounts use paper checks—slips of paper with bank information on it that you can use as money at stores and other places you buy things.

People can also open a savings account at a bank or credit union. You can actually earn money through interest that the bank or credit union offers. Interest is money that the financial institution puts into your account as sort of a thank you for storing your money with them.

When Wimee and his friends had questions about money, they knew they could ask a trusted adult—their neighbor Mr. Bill. If you have more questions about money, ask a trusted adult in your life such as a family member, librarian, or teacher. Happy learning!